THE BEARS' CHRISTMAS

THE BEARS' CHRISTMAS

By
Stan and Jan
Berenstain

BEGINNER BOOKS   A Division of Random House, Inc.

This title was originally catalogued by the Library of Congress as follows: Berenstain, Stanley. The bears' Christmas, by Stan and Jan Berenstain. [New York] Beginner Books [1970] 59 p. col. illus. 24 cm. Daddy Bear tries to show his son how to use the sled, skates, and skis Santa brought for Christmas. "B-55." [1. Winter sports—Stories. 2. Christmas stories. 3. Stories in rhyme] I. Berenstain, Janice joint author. II. Title. PZ8.3.B4493Bc [E] 79-117542 ISBN 0-394-80090-7 ISBN 0-394-90090-1 (lib. bdg.)

THE BEARS' CHRISTMAS

Merry Christmas, Son!
I see Santa was here.
Did he bring you
what you asked for this year?

Yes, Dad. Look!

He brought me all these!

A sled! And some skates!

And he brought me some skis.

6

This will be the best Christmas
you ever had.
I'll teach you
to use these things.
Follow your Dad!

Let's try the sled first.
Let's try the sled here.

8

No.

I know a better place.

This is too near.

The best place to sled
is up there.
Up ahead.

I learned to sled there
when I was a kid.
Wait till I show you
the things that I did.

Now watch what I do.
Keep your eye on your Pop.
The first thing to learn
is my Great Belly Flop.

First

I hold the sled high.

Then I start to run.

Then I flop on my belly.

That's how it is done.

Wow!

That's really something, Pop!

Is that the way to Belly Flop?

17

Thank you, Dad,
for showing me how.
Give me my sled
and I'll Belly Flop now.

19

Not now, my son.
It's getting late.
I still have to teach you
to ski and to skate.

21

My friends used to call me
The Great Skating Bear.
And I'll show you why
on that ice down there.

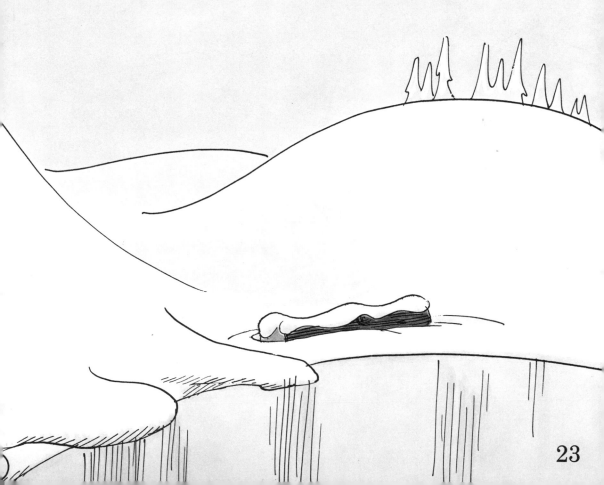

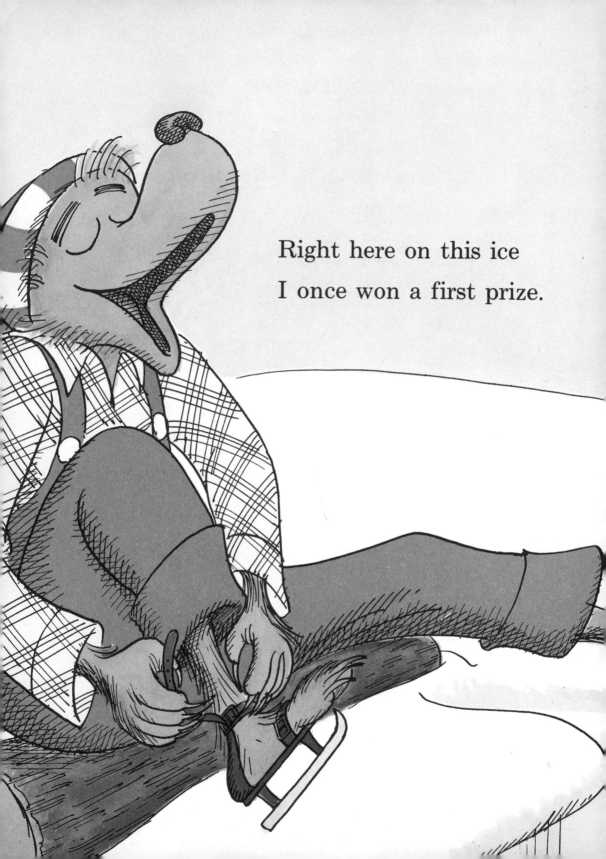

Right here on this ice
I once won a first prize.

But my skates don't fit you.
They're not the right size.

I won the first prize
for my Great Figure Eight.
And here's how I did it.
On only one skate!

28

See! Half of my Great
Figure Eight is all done.
Now comes the second half.
Watch me, my son.

31

Thank you, Dad,

for showing me how.

I think I know all about

ice skating now.

There's a place over here
where you can sit.
You can warm up,
and I'll practice a bit.

36

Look, Pa! I'm skating!
I'm pretty keen.
Look, Pa! I'm doing
a Figure Sixteen!

38

That wasn't too bad.

You're learning, I see.

But now come along.

Now I'll teach you to ski.

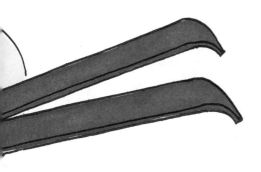

Here's my old ski jump.
We'll ride to the top
and you'll get a lesson
from Ski Jumper Pop.

When you first put on skis,

be careful. Don't slip.

And watch where you're going.

Be sure you don't trip.

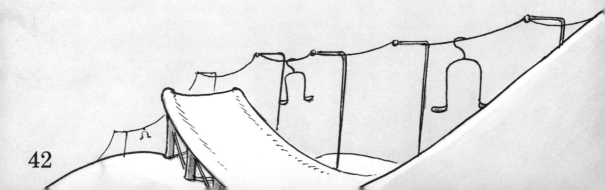

I'm watching! I'm watching!
But tell me, Pop, please . . .
Are you going to go jumping
without any skis?

Don't ask silly questions.

Just do as I say.

Just follow me down,

and I'll show you the way.

49

Well, I've had enough
of this Christmas Day fun.
How would you like to
go home now, my son?

Hi, Ma! We're back!
Doesn't Papa look nice?
All wrapped up for Christmas
in nice snow and ice.

Thank you, Dad. Thank you.
Your lessons were great.
I learned how to ski,
how to sled, how to skate.

It's our best Christmas ever.

Don't you think so, Dad?

Yes.

The very best Christmas

we ever have had!